The Letter

For All Those Who Believe in Love,
Soul Mates, and Forever

Dan Clark

Order this book online at www.trafford.com
or email orders@trafford.com

Most Trafford titles are also available at major online book retailers.

Printed in Victoria, BC, Canada.

ISBN: 978-1-4269-1799-8 (soft)

Library of Congress Control Number: 2009936398

*Our mission is to efficiently provide the world's finest, most comprehensive book publishing
service, enabling every author to experience success. To find out how to publish your book, your
way, and have it available worldwide, visit us online at www.trafford.com*

Trafford rev. 11/03/09

www.trafford.com

North America & international
toll-free: 1 888 232 4444 (USA & Canada)
phone: 250 383 6864 ✦ fax: 812 355 4082

PREFACE

From the time we are born we have an innate feeling that we belong to something or to someone. The idea of a soul mate or even eternal love is romantic, it is mysterious, and in many cases, it is reality. The metaphysician believes in the eternity of the soul. That soul, born prior to earthly life and lasting long after this life is over, feels, believes, thinks and can mature. Is it so far from reality then that the soul can also love?

"The Letter" is a story of that simple eternal love. Through the relationship of Elaine and Brad one explores the idea of eternal soul mate love and the realization that the most difficult aspect of love is the ability to recognize it.

To then be worthy of it and to make every sacrifice available to enjoy the sweetness and serenity of that God like gift to all of us is our destiny.

It is my wish that you, dear reader, find and recognize your own eternal love. I hope you enjoy reading "The Letter".

DEDICATION

This book is dedicated to the soul mate who continues to touch my life in every way.

PROLOG

There was a time our souls embraced
your eyes and mine were one.
our words, in concert, filled the sky
and cooled the blistering sun.
Our future written by the Gods
was bright and full of hope,
the love we shared brought majesty to every flame we stoked.

Oh, how remiss the fates have been, to cause this great divide
no longer are our souls entwined,
no longer side by side.

The path that took you far from me
has left a trail of tears.
The suffering of the soul, the anguished cry of fear.
Eternal life, a dream of mine, shone brightly
through the mist.
But now, without your love,
it is nothing but a wish.

So hopeless is the reckoning of prior god's consent
that hope of love with you my dear
is now completely spent.
Alone I walk, the futures there, the life that I must face
Oh, how I wish there'd come a time,
our souls would re-embrace.

FORWARD

It is a typical Seattle morning with the rain drizzling lightly, the sky gray and Elaine is settling in for a very routine day. Little does she know that this day would be anything but ordinary? Today she receives "the letter".

Brad, who has travelled the world and back again, could never get Elaine out of his mind or heart. He knows she has been married and he also knows that almost thirty years ago he was hopelessly in love with her. So much has happened. Even his innate spiritual powers could not help him out of this one. He had to write "the letter" and see what would evolve.

This idea of loving someone for so many years and having them come back to you is idealized romance. If it does happen then it happens at the most inopportune of times.

Needless to say, people change so that person is going to be different. Well, unless the love they shared originally was spiritual in nature. You see, the spirit is forever and while it matures its' essence does not change. It is in that knowledge that one finds comfort.

Now Brad has written the letter and Elaine has received it. Can they find the secret for lasting eternal love? Or do they let this chance pass them by?

Chapter 1

July 2008

So she finally had time to do what she had put off for far too long. As she stared at it, sitting there with all the other correspondence: bills to pay, cards, advertisements, magazines; she knew it was time. She heard a noise outside and her eyes moved wistfully to a flock of birds flying over the sound as if there was a respite from the task ahead.

Elaine loved Puget Sound. The smell of the rain and the pine trees had always been one of her favorite aromas. When she was a small girl her father had taken her family to the mountains in the spring. Everything was fresh and new and she felt so close to nature. Looking over the aqua blue colors of the sound contrasting to the green of the pine strewn hills took her back to those childhood days. She often longed for the simplicity and innocence of that time. My, how time have changed!

Elaine was married now with children of her own. This was her second marriage, and while comfortable, it was not the passion or unity that she imagined. She recalled that as a child she had dreamt of that one perfect prince charming moment. The handsome man who would ride into her life and change it completely! She thought it would be an eternal love, a soul mate even. Yet today, both her marriages had not reached that lofty expectation. Not that she was unhappy, just disappointed that life was so unrelenting. She often questioned the very existence of a soul mate. Though she had heard that many people believed in them, she was having difficulty believing in that idea ever since she was 19 years old.

Now, she brought her eyes back into the room and her attention back to the moment.

She looked at the envelope again, slowly reached her hand forward and plucked it from the stack. How many times had she done the very same thing? Over and over it seemed. She just didn't know. This time, however, was different. Instead of just reading it, she would take time to respond. It was finally time to resolve it all. It was time to answer "the letter".

Chapter 2

The letter arrived on a Thursday morning almost seven months ago. Elaine recalled the day perfectly. It was a typical Seattle morning with the green of the pines clashing with the murky blue waters of the Pacific Ocean. She lingered a moment at the kitchen window as she watched the slithering mist rising from the water do battle with the constant drizzle flowing from the heavy gray clouds above. It seemed to always rain in Seattle, even though it only rained in the mornings. The rain was winning this battle which was not unusual. While beautiful; the colors, the smells and yes, even the rain, she felt depressed. It seemed that the weather always did that. She conveniently blamed the weather, just like everyone else who lived in the Pacific Northwest. She certainly couldn't say it was the routine of her life that caused her depression. And it wasn't for missed opportunities that had passed away untouched. So in her mind, the weather was the perfect culprit.

It seems that her life had become very predictable! Her husband was away at work like every other day. Quite successful in his own business, Dave provided well for the family. She had fallen in like with him early in the relationship and thought that love would come. She still harbored warm feelings and felt closer to him today than 20 years ago, but something was missing, that special feeling just wasn't there. Maybe it wasn't supposed to be. Her mother had found her true love and seemed to enjoy a marriage full of love and passion. Why, Elaine wondered, was it so difficult for her to have that same happiness?

The kids were in school. Both had grown into fine young adults. The youngest, a beautiful girl was now attending the University of Washington studying medicine. The oldest was a senior in Southern California and was looking forward to a career in paleontology. Elaine was proud of both of them although she had to admit that she wasn't sure where the paleontology came from.

Today Elaine had called in sick from work. She had been a cashier at the supermarket for over 25 years. She started when she was just 18 and shortly after beginning work she met her first husband in the same store where she worked. She always thought it was destiny to meet your partner in the frozen food area. Elaine smiled as she recalled the episode of Happy Days where Fonze was telling Richie that the best place to find a date was at the supermarket. She wasn't sure about the date thing but it certainly was a good place to find a husband. Now though she really wondered if it was her destiny. Destiny, fate, even forever love ran through her mind. These were phrases and thoughts that she didn't even think about until a boyfriend named Brad taught her about them.

So for all those reasons, she stayed. It was a very routine job but a good one where, at least, she felt needed. The same people came in every week. They always bought the same items. They were always either sad, or happy, rushed or not, alone or with the kids or occasionally with the partner of the week. Then there was Mrs. Wilson. Yes she was different. She was a lovely 80 year old lady who seemed to have conquered the world. Always a smile and a good word came from her. Elaine recalled one conversation where Mrs. Wilson talked about her soul mate. She missed him terribly but knew she would be reunited with him in the end. That belief brought her much joy. Elaine wanted so much to have that same belief, but her life had taken her away from that. Reality was that you date a lot of people and find one or maybe two and finally get married. Marriage is a ton of work. It requires sacrifice and a lot of give and take. Nothing is easy. Because of that, why would anyone want to be with someone forever?

Today though no work just a lazy day at home. Dave was away, the kids gone and all she was going to do was clean the house, read a little and talk with her mom. In fact her mother called around 10:00 that morning and they had discussed everything from church to the kids to her mother's new hobby, macramé. But nothing about Elaine, nothing about her life, her boredom and her wishing that something exciting would happen, just for a change.

At 12:00 o'clock she sat down to finish reading a book about soul mates and true love.

Stories of star crossed lovers had always appealed to her. She wondered if true love really did exist, and if it did, why, at least in stories and movies, it never lasted. As she turned to page 116, the door bell rang. She rose from the couch and walked slowly to the door. Her surprise at seeing the DHL delivery boy was muted although she was curious. She hadn't ordered anything via mail and she was sure that her husband Dave hadn't either. As she signed for the letter and glanced for a return address the delivery boy said,

"Wow, it must be nice to know someone from overseas?"

It seemed more like a question, but she could not answer it because she didn't have an answer. In her life she had known several people that had lived overseas. But that was a long time ago and recently her friends had been made at church, the supermarket or with her husband. And they were all local.

She closed the front door and returned to her couch. As she sank back into the same sitting place as before, her blue eyes roamed over the outside of the package for a clue. There was nothing there. Her heart skipped a beat and she was confused. What was her heart telling her? The address said Tokyo, but she knew no one in Tokyo. She started to open the package. As she reached inside she retrieved a legal sized white envelope. There was a return address on it! It was from somewhere in Texas. There was a name......Stevens.

She stared at the name and her mind began to wander. The only Stevens she had ever known, well the only important one, was a young boy of 16. A young man that had come into her life so surprisingly and one that had impacted her life so profoundly that the six months they had spent together she had felt more alive than ever in her life. But that was almost 30 years ago. And as far as she knew he never lived in Texas, and even if he did go to Japan for two years earlier in his life, he certainly didn't know where she lived or to whom she had gotten married or anything else about her. How could he? She had been married twice. The first time was a six month mistake and done, now that she thought about it, because he had gotten married first. Damn him anyway. The memories were starting to come back.

Chapter 3
October 1969

"Hey Elaine, have you seen this poem that that weird kid Brad wrote?" Terri asked. Terrie was a short pixie-ish girl with a nose for everything. Brad was the boy with the reputation from the other church group. He and his family had recently arrived in Teri and Elaine's group because the Elders had relined the boundaries of the different chapels. Now this trouble maker was in Teri's group and she did not like it at all.

Teri was a typical teenage girl. She loved boys and talking but she also didn't like change. Brad represented change. She wasn't sure if it was a premonition, omen or just teenage hormones, but she was worried that something was going to change forever and she didn't like that feeling at all.

"Teri, why do you think he is weird? You don't even know him?" Elaine replied with a smile."

"That's true. But you have heard the same thing I have. He is a loud mouth, makes jokes during class and he believes in strange things like seers, soul mates, and talking to God."

"And, so what? Don't you pray to God yourself? And what is wrong with the idea of soul mates? I think it is kind of romantic." Elaine thought to herself how nice it would be to actually have a partner forever.

"Besides, don't you think we should give him a chance? Let me see the poem, please"

Teri reluctantly handed the poem over to Elaine. Teri and Elaine had been friends since sixth grade. Now as they embarked upon the teenage years, Elaine was the same sweet innocent girl she had always been only now she was tall, blond and beautiful. It would be easy to be jealous of Elaine but she was such a real and genuine person that everyone loved her.

Elaine took the poem and began to read.

Forever Love

it touches what cannot be touched
and strives to reach those aspects not far removed
from whence we began
but not today, nor even on the morrow
would we question what remains.

the grace of you,
your eyes reveal and man has stated often
the portals to the soul and yet they know
your soul is more than what they seek
and more than I have learned to understand

our spirits touched so long ago,
before this mortal life
and all the lives we lived before
were but a moment lingering
for today we find the reality of it all

lest we forget our past
a thousand years together
the paths we travel here today
are nothing more than dreams
for you and I have always been exactly what we are

inseparable from birth to death
and no matter who might interfere
their moments are not blessed
nor can they impact hearts that are sworn
one to the other

there are no star crossings that could affect
that which is shared so deeply
the spirits touch, the hearts are one
and pretenders can postpone
but not derail

Elaine had to take a moment to reread it. It was hard for her to understand how a boy of 16 could write something so beautiful. The poem seemed to call to her. She needed to get to know this young man. Anyone who could write with such heart had to be special.

Elaine read the poem again.

"Teri, can I keep this?" she asked

"Oh, oh," Teri replied. "I sense a problem here." And with a loud giggle, Teri relinquished the poem to Elaine.

Elaine took the poem and when she got home she sat on her bed and read it over again. Something in her heart told her that this was special. Elaine had always listened to her heart. Even as a young girl, most of her decisions were made with the heart and not the mind. Her mother had taught her that the heart is the most pure organ of the body. It was that part of the body directly linked to God. Anytime she felt alone, she could turn to her heart and god's love would lighten her way.

Her heart was talking to her now but she didn't have a clue what it was saying. She folded the poem and as she put it away, she said to herself, "I guess I better get ready for this ride."

Chapter 4

July 2008

She gazed at the letter. Her long finger, perfectly manicured, sliding its way across the top from one side to another. So many questions! Well maybe the letter would provide the answers. She opened it and began to read:

Dear Elaine,

I know this will be a surprise for you. I hope it is a nice one. My sister just sent some photos to me from my parent's house. Unfortunately, both mom and dad have passed away. It was last year when first my dad and then my mother passed on. I felt bad not being there but work in Tokyo has been very busy and both deaths were quite sudden. Do you remember that my father was in the Air Force? Well, he had just retired about two years earlier. What a shame to not be able to enjoy your retirement. And they had just built a home in Utah.

Mom lasted about seven months after that. It was longer than I thought she would. They are now both together again. The nice thing was that my sister Marie was still living close and could take care of the arrangements.

Paul, my brother, (do you remember?), was also close. He took care of all the religious arrangements. I understand it was a nice service.

Well, anyway, Marie was going through their things when she ran across several photos of me and my friends. One was a picture of a 14 year old girl with long blond hair and blue eyes. I have to admit it brought back many memories. All of them good, by the way, as you would probably expect. I wanted to write and say thank you. You came into my life at the right time and helped me through my difficult teenage years. While my mom may have thought I was obsessed, I still think it was love. And your love helped me turn out much better than I could have hoped. So, THANK YOU.

Anyway, I am sure that you are happy and still living in the Pacific Northwest. I was sorry to hear about your first marriage ending as it did, but understand that you are content in your present situation. I am happy for you and hope that this letter does not change that which does not need to be changed. I am sure that this will be a surprise for you. The confusion should be interesting. I am sending this from Tokyo, where, can you believe it? After so many years I have moved back here for a job with Bank of the World. Life is a complete circle isn't it? Who would have thought that my missionary work when I was 21 to Japan would come back and help me in my career? The return address on the envelope is for my home in Texas, because I still have to come back to the states sometime. That should be interesting. Maybe someday you can visit. With your family of course!

Well, I'd better let you go. Don't feel that you have to respond to this letter (although a Christmas card would be nice). But other than that there is no need because

I know our paths will cross again. They always seem to, don't they?

Well take care and God's Speed

Love,

Brad

It was such a short letter, but it said so much. She laid it down, went to the kitchen to fix some tea, an orange mint fusion, and then stopped and put on some music. She settled back down. The aroma of the tea was perfect for the day and the music began to play. She remembered thinking, why did it have to be Manilow?

She picked up the letter and read it again. This time more slowly. Her heart was still beating fast, she began to tingle all over and there was that certain feeling happening to her all over again. She knew it well. It had occurred the first time she met Brad and now, almost thirty years later it was happening all over again. The memories began to flow.

Chapter 5

October 1969

Elaine was getting ready for church. She had an important task ahead today. She was going to have her cousin introduce her to the new boy, Brad. True, her boyfriend of the moment Bill would not like it, but there was something about the poem she had read that told her she needed to speak to the new boy.

Because his dad was in the Air Force, he lived on base and attended High School. Church was the only place that she would be able to talk to him. This was foolhardy and she knew it. The Air Force, all the military in fact, moved people in and out so fast your head would spin. Why would anyone want to get involved with someone like that? But that poem!

A smile came to her lips when she thought about her parents. Dad would object of course, but mom, well she was different. Elaine actually thought her mother might like Brad. She always sided with Elaine anyway but this time might be a difficult challenge for dear old mom. If Elaine's heart was true then this Brad could be someone very special for her. Elaine knew her mother would be very protective and question why at such a young age would someone feel so strongly for another person?

Besides, when she told her parents everything about Brad, it might get a bit difficult. She had heard that Brad protested the war in Vietnam.

She had heard that he was arrested and his parents were really upset. Truth was, as it turned out, he had attended a sit-in for peace and his parents never even knew about it. He was never arrested and while he supported the young people fighting the war he was against violence. He was also against guns, and while not fully focused on the peace movement, Brad always thought that a peaceful solution to problems was the best solution.

Arriving at church and getting out of the car she looked for Mike her cousin. He was talking with Bill and Elaine walked up to them both.

"Good morning guys. Mike, can I talk to you for a minute?" Bill, give us a few moments okay? Thanks." Elaine smiled and took Mike by the hand to a safe distance. After all she didn't want to hurt Bill's feelings.

"Mike, I want you to introduce me to that new boy Brad."

"Excuse me!" Mike look bewildered as he spoke the words. "You have to be crazy!"

"Maybe, bet even so, I want you to introduce me. You do know him, don't you? From school? Please?" Elaine half begged because she knew Mike would do it.

"But what about Bill" Mike asked?

Bill had been Mike's best friend for several months and had been Elaine's boyfriend for the last three weeks. Bill was completely smitten but Elaine was indifferent.

"I will talk to him right now. This is something I need to do. Don't ask me why, I just have this feeling."

"You do know that he believes in witches and weird things like that?" Mike said. "You better be careful or he will turn you into a frog princess." Mike laughed at his own sense of humor, and pointing a finger at Elaine pretended to change her into a frog.

"No he doesn't. He believes in eternal love, in soul mates and the metaphysical world is all. I think it is interesting. Besides he writes really well." Elaine smiled at her cousin with that mischievous twinkle in her eye. Mike knew then that it was hopeless.

"OK, OK, right after class!" Mike went back to Bill.

"Bill, Elaine wants to talk to you." Mike watched as Bill began talking with Elaine and continued to watch as Elaine gently let Bill know that she was going to move on to other things. Bill's head dropped and he said goodbye.

Sunday school class couldn't get over fast enough for Elaine. Finally she walked out of class and headed to the double doors leading to the parking lot. She knew Mike would have Brad there by now and she wanted to meet this mystery boy.

As she opened the door and walked out to the newly trimmed hedge she saw Mike talking to Brad. They both looked in her direction and began to walk over. Elaine began to tingle and a peaceful aura covered her completely. It was so strong that she didn't know what to do. When Brad moved his hand forward to greet her, she froze. Then with a smile she said,

"Hi, I'm Elaine. You must be Brad. It is a pleasure to meet you."

They shook hands. Very polite, she thought, but unusual. He had a great smile, his touch was electric and even though he wasn't the handsomest of boys, his eyes had power. His strength lay in his eyes and knowing this she knew that she had found the one for her.

As Brad started to talk, he heard "Bradley, it's time to go". Brad turned around and smiled, said a quick goodbye and walked towards his parents. It would be another week before he would be able to talk to Elaine.

She went home totally confused. She was fourteen and he was sixteen. They could not date, she was too young, and they would only see each other on Sundays and maybe once in a while during the week. He went to High School and she to Junior High. He was also the son of an Air Force Officer so she knew he was going to leave. They all did. Yes the confusion was great, but the peace of mind and heart were stronger and she allowed herself to commit.

The week passed by quickly and before they knew it Sunday had arrived. This time Elaine went straight up to Brad, took his hand and they sat together throughout the service. "Just so you know," she said, "I am yours and you are mine." Elaine looked at Brad with a smile and twinkle in her eye. Brad was hooked.

Elaine was never this assertive but there was something about the boy that made her feel completely at home.

This time the couple actually had some time after church to talk and get to know each other.

"So, Brad. Where did you learn to write poetry? " Elaine asked.

"I'm not sure Elaine. My mom says that I have a grandma who used to write quite well. I think that it is a nice idea but she could not have passed on her talent to me because I was adopted into this family when I was only 4 years old."

"Really, I didn't know that. Tell me about your real parents. Do you know them?"

Elaine was curious to find out everything about this person.

"Yes I do. My mother writes at least twice a year. She lives in Germany. My father was a soldier whom she met right after the war. Apparently my mom was a little liberal when it came to men and did not get married even though she was pregnant with me. She seems like a very nice lady though. And my parents here are nice. We move around a lot because of dad's work, but it is fun. I seem to have adjusted to that life pretty well. But tell me about you."

"Well, first, here my phone number so you can call me. I don't want to wait until Sunday to talk with you. I have lived here all my life. Dad has a store that he built from scratch and he has done well. I have a little sister who's a brat, but I love her." She smiled.

"My mom is really special. You will need to meet her. I think she will like you." Elaine smiled at that very thought.

Brad thought at that moment that he would never forget that smile. It was a smile that made the angels sing!

"Well I have got to go, Brad. Maybe someday you will write me a poem. Did you know that no one wanted you to come to our church? You had a bad reputation. Well, nobody but me."

She smiled again, gave him a kiss on the cheek and was gone.

Brad stood there watching her leave. A kiss? Bad reputation? Everyone but her? This was one strange girl.

Write her a poem. Gee, maybe some day. But then he realized, as he thought about it, he already had.

"Let's go Bradley."

Brad turned and walked to his sister and on to the car. Another week and Elaine had begun to get to him.

Chapter 6
December 1969

Christmas was fast approaching. Elaine and Brad had been together for three months. It was amazing how quickly Brad adjusted to the new church group. And the reputation he supposedly had was just a memory. He was not sure if it was that people got to know him or if it was his relationship with Elaine. No matter, he and Elaine were the young couple of the moment.

Brad would often play piano during church and Elaine would direct the choir. They both taught a children's class, together. The older members of the group walked away quite impressed with young love. These two young people, quite unremarkable separately, had transformed into, well, he was not really sure, but they were special.

Even his mother was coming around. At the beginning of the relationship she had frowned upon Brad being dedicated to only one girl, especially one of 14 years of age. But Elaine had won her over. Elaine was much more mature than her age indicated and Lidia knew when she saw her son and Elaine together that there was magic. That's why she actually helped them see each other.

Lidia was in charge of the Christmas youth dance this year. It was for youth over the age of 16, so Bradley was going. Unfortunately Elaine was too young and so was not invited. Brad was reluctant to go but

Elaine told him that he needed to be with his friends. "Just don't dance with anyone else" she ribbed him.

"Bradley," Lidia started to question, "Who could you recommend to help me at the Christmas dance? I need someone in the kitchen and to help with refreshments. Your sister is at school and I don't know anyone other than Elaine. Do you think she would mind?

"Gee mom, I am sure she wouldn't mind. Do you want me to call her?"

"No dear, I will talk to her mother."

And as simple as that, Elaine was at the dance. However there was a problem. Seemed that with Brad and Elaine in the kitchen helping Lidia that all the other kids ended up in the kitchen too! It wasn't too long before Lidia took Elaine's hand, placed it in Brad's and said "you two go dance. I can't have all you kids in here all the time." "And by the way take all your friends with you."

Brad and Elaine led the troupe to the dance floor and no one even remembered that Elaine wasn't even 16. By the time the party was over everyone had had a great time, and Brad and Elaine were in love.

"Elaine," Brad asked, "do you remember when we met and you said that someday I could write a poem for you?"

"Yes Brad, I do. Did you finally get inspired?" Elaine smirked with the twinkle in her eye, knowing that she would win this conversation.

"Well not really inspired?" started Brad. Elaine feigned sadness and disappointment with a frown and Brad quickly said "Hah, finally got you. You know I am kidding, of course you inspire me."

Elaine smiled and said, "Sorry Brad but I have always known I was your inspiration, so I got you!"

They both laughed and fell into each others arms. Elaine always felt so secure with Brad like this. There was nothing sexual about it, just simple, innocent and complete.

"Well, yes Elaine, you did inspire me. Here is a poem just for you. But please don't read it until you get home. I don't want to see your face if you don't like it."

Elaine smiled, gave Brad a quick squeeze of the hand and took the folded paper from him. She could hardly wait to get home and read the poem.

Once home, Elaine went right to her room and unfolded the poem. She began to read.

Spirit

She walks upon the clouds of joy
and leaves them bright with love
and yet she touches not your soul
nor can she dream because
no matter where the rays of light
reside at final rest
to be within that which is lost
can only cause detest

The spirit sighs with inward eyes
toward unyielding wants
while solace in the sapphire moon
provides resulting taunts
we can not tell nor can we speak
of things that yet have passed
but can you feel, in moment's wings
your history not re-massed

It swirls round the misty breech
caressing what it finds
and being of the body's soul
there is no peace of mind

because the thoughts that drive you there
will often lead astray
hence where we came is where we go
and here is where we stay

Dream often child and drift apart
from human misery
lift eyes toward the satin sun
and heart towards the breeze
the spirit leads to where it goes
and you will often find
a spirits touch will heal the past
and bring you peace of mind.

Elaine put the paper down. She thought for a moment and then re read the poem. It seemed to talk of a tortured soul finding peace. Did Brad write it for me or was I his inspiration to reflect on his own struggles. It seemed to reflect her inner most thoughts; those very thoughts that she kept hidden from everyone because they might be misinterpreted. Yet Brad had found them and it only took a few months. Elaine was scared for the first time in her life. How could a person read so much from my soul? Is he a witch? But then, as she reached for the phone, her spirit was engulfed by a peaceful serenity. It was so strong that she put the phone down, decided to call Brad tomorrow and fell asleep. She couldn't wait to dream.

Chapter 7
December 1969

Elaine awoke early the next day. The dream was vivid and alive in her mind. She went downstairs and looking through the house, found her mother at the kitchen table.

"Mom," Elaine started, "can I talk to you about something?"

"Why of course dear. You know that we can talk about anything. What is it?" Susan asked.

Susan was a beautiful woman. She had a spirit that seemed to ooze from every pore of her body with light and love. Mother Goose, Mother Nature and every good image of a woman you can imagine seemed to all reside within this one person. Giving and patient, loving and kind, Susan was a wonderful role model for Elaine, and loved her daughters very much. She also knew her daughters very intimately. More than being a birth mother, Susan was the spiritual birth mother of both the girls although none of them understood it at the time.

"Brad gave me this poem last night. Then I had a dream. I wondered if we could talk about them both." Elaine pleaded, with a bit of sadness in her eyes.

Susan was not used to seeing Elaine with any sort of sadness. She was concerned and dropped what she was doing. Taking Elaine by the hand, they went onto the patio and sat down.

"Elaine, may I read the poem?

Elaine handed her mother the poem and sat quietly while Susan read it. When finished, Susan turned to her daughter and said simply, "This young man really understands you, doesn't he? But that doesn't surprise me. Please tell me about your dream."

"Well Mom, what I remember is that I was in the sky. There was a long skywalk that led from cloud to cloud. I followed the skywalk and in the distance I saw a beautiful city in the clouds. It was so beautiful. Pure white nestled in the clouds of purple and red and blue. As I entered the city I noticed that everything was organized perfectly with the streets paved in white brick and cleaner than anything I ever saw. There were people everywhere but I could not make out any faces and didn't seem to know any of them. The clouds were multi colored and billowy and the city sat upon the largest of them.

I walked around the city and noticed a crowd gathering in an arena type of building. It was large like an auditorium at a college, but more ornate. It was made of white marble and there was gold trim. Everyone who entered was dressed in white robes. When I looked down at myself, I too was wearing a white robe.

Everyone was entering this building and I asked someone what was this all about. He told me that the Master was talking to everyone. It was going to be a wonderful message. I got in line to hear the message and an usher came up to me and asked to see a certain mark on my shoulder. I showed him my shoulder but there was no mark there and he kindly told me that I was not chosen for this message yet. He said that I had a mission to complete.

I was confused and asked him what he meant.

He told me that there was someplace that God wanted me to go to and a person I had to find. He said the person needed me. I asked him who it was and he told me that he could not tell me but that I would know. He said it was my destiny to be with that person for all time and eternity".

"The only thing that I know," he said, "is that you will know when you find him."

"Can you tell me anything else?" I said.

"Only that he is your soul mate and he needs you and you him to be complete and ease your pain."

"I then was walking on the earth going towards a school and I woke up."

"What do you think it all means mom?" Elaine was perplexed and fearful.

Susan could see the angst within her daughter's soul and smiled gently at the young woman who had just had a spiritual awakening.

"Elaine, my dear daughter, you have always been so special. Your father and I have loved you from the moment you were conceived. And every day of you life we have grown to love you more. However I have always known that there was always emptiness in your life."

"Really, mom?" Elaine asked. "But I haven't felt any emptiness."

"It's is a specific emptiness that you have. Take a look at the poem Brad wrote. It is about that emptiness. See the following lines:"

nor can she dream because
no matter where the rays of light
reside at final rest
to be within that which is lost
can only cause detest

"Brad is talking about what you have lost. It is so subtle that most people never really feel it. And even fewer recognize the loss. I am surprised that Brad has seen it in you. But then again, I don't know why I would be surprised. He is a remarkable young man."

"Wow, mom, you really think so. I always thought you and dad didn't like him." Elaine sounded confused.

"It's not that we don't like him dear, it is that it surprised us he arrived so quickly into your life."

"What do you mean mom? Was all this planned?"

"It appears so. I think I should tell you about eternal love and soul mates. I think you may have found your twin flame. Your dream confirms it to me.

Susan got up from the table and turned off the phone. This was once when she wanted no interruptions. Elaine was in for a long struggle with this twin flame of hers and Susan wanted to make sure that Elaine understood the secret.

She took her daughter to the back patio and as they sat down Susan told Elaine,

"Many people look down on the idea of soul mates, twin flames and eternal love. That always surprised me because they talk about wanting to love someone forever and yet they get married "until death do we part". When approached with the idea that love could last forever, almost everyone thinks it is a great romantic idea. Very few people will admit that there is such a thing."

Elaine slid closer to her mother and listened intently.

"Before we are born, we have a spirit. Its shape and form are not important, but let us say that our spirits look just like we do today, only not in solid form. Well, these spirits think and move, they feel and they grow. But they can only grow so much in that world. You see

Elaine, there are things that spirits can not do. They can not feel in the physical sense, nor can they procreate. That is the reason that we must all come to this planet and obtain a body. That way the spirit will better be able to understand the limitations of the physical body as well as the blessings of having children. Do you see?"

Elaine said she did and Susan continued.

"Your dream was prompted by the poem Brad wrote you. The City was heaven and the reason it was so beautiful, clean and white is that it was pure and spiritual. The people going to see the Master were pairs weren't they?" Susan asked.

"Now that you mention it, yes they were. They all looked so happy and content and much alike mom. I couldn't tell who was who because they looked like one person. But I know that there were two people in line." Elaine replied.

"Yes dear. They were two and one. They were soul mates. Soul mates are people who from the beginning of time were each part of the others life. They were promised that they could learn different lessons here on earth. God promised that they would find each other again, and once they did, would accomplish great works here on this planer. Twin Flames are special soul mates. These are souls that were paired prior to birth. They complete each other and because they were born of love, their love can overcome any obstacle. God promised them that they would be able to recognize themselves and join together. Then they would learn the secrets of true happiness because they would be complete. These couples in your dream were going to learn that secret. You couldn't enter because you had not found your twin flame yet. The dream confirms that you have one and you must search him out. That is your mission in life."

"Gee mom, this is so interesting. How will I know who my soul mate is and what about my twin flame and what will happen to us if we don't find each other?" Elaine asked in quick abandon. So many questions were coming to her now.

"Well dear, we will always find our twin flame. It may be early or it may be late. It may be over several years. It may be in another lifetime altogether. Soul mates arrive when they are needed. They could be in your own family, a close friend or even a business partner. They come when you need the spiritual support and they leave when you have passed the difficult part of your life. Twin flames seem to arrive and return until the recognition takes place.

For example, did I ever tell you that I met your dad when I was six years old?"

"Really, Mom, I had no idea. What happened?"

"We were at a church meeting and he pulled my hair. I knew in that moment he was my soul mate. I didn't see him again for 5 years and then again after college. Neither one of us had found anyone else and had not been in love. Then, when we saw each other that last year of college, a light went off. We both knew why we hadn't fallen for anyone else. So you see Elaine, our paths crossed several different times and in the end we ended up together."

"My thought dear is that Brad touched your soul with his insightful poem and that his writing it is a sign to you that he is the one. Obviously, I am not telling you anything that you don't already know am I?" Susan asked with a smile and that same twinkle in her eye that her daughter had inherited.

"No mom, it's nothing new. I have known from the moment I heard his name. He is my soul mate. I do love him so."

The tears began to well up in Elaine's eyes. Her mother embraced her and held her close.

It is a difficult moment when you are only 14 years old yet know that your soul mate has arrived. Susan held Elaine close, knowing the pain that she was going to suffer before she found eternal peace and happiness.

Chapter 8

April 1970

It was a beautiful spring day in Tacoma Washington. Brad was with his friend at high school. They were sitting under a tree enjoying the sun and solving the world's problems.

Of course they should have been in class as the Vice Principle advised them when he came upon them 15 minutes after the last bell.

"Okay you three. Get to class. What are you doing here anyway?"

Brad responded for the group,

"We are discussing social events like the war and what it means to us as we get older."

"Well how about you discuss that in your class. And by the way, tell your teacher that you deserve a red "F" for the day."

As the three of them walked back to class, they advised Ms. Scott that the Vice Principle had told them to let her know that deserved a "red F" for the day. One by one the three of them walked slowly to her desk where she pulled out a red pen and asking each to place their hand, palm down on the desk, took the pen and marked each hand with a red F.

"There," she said. "That should take of that."

Ms. Scott was always the best teacher. She never took anything so seriously as to ruin the creativity of her students. That is why they all loved her. And she loved all of them especially Brad and his two friends. Not only were they good students, they were leaders of the class and did what was the right thing to do.

Brad however, had a disconcerting feeling that day. He couldn't quite place his finger on it, but something wasn't quite right. He was doing okay in all his classes. His piano lessons were great and Elaine was, well, Elaine was Elaine. He had never been happier.

Yet there was an unsettling feeling in the depths of his soul. He wondered what it was.

When Brad got home he noticed his father was home as well. This was not normal because Brad always got home first.

"Hey Dad, what's up?" Brad asked almost absent mindedly.

"Come on in Brad." Colonel Stevens ordered. Brad's father was a good man but being military everything seemed to be an order with him. So Brad went in and sat down.

"Brad, I need to tell you that we are going to have to leave Tacoma."

There was nothing as heart breaking as hearing those words. Brad began to realize the meaning of his restlessness and his loss.

"They are closing the squadron down and we can go to either Alaska or North Dakota. I have opted for North Dakota. I am sure you will be supportive of this move."

Brad wasn't listening now; something about Alaska and cold weather. They were leaving Tacoma; his friends, his school, his sports. He was leaving Elaine. He couldn't leave Elaine.

"Are you sure dad? Do we have to go?" Brad's sister asked as if reading Brad's mind.

"Yes Marie, we have to go. I have my orders. But we have a week, so that will give us time to say goodbye to all our friends and enjoy this weather a little longer.

Brad got up and called Elaine.

Chapter 9

July 2008

Their relationship had lasted eight months. It was wonderfully rewarding, spiritually fulfilling and represented, even today, the best of her life. She recalled the discovery that he was not such a bad boy after all. In fact they had become the perfect couple at church.

When he spoke at church, which is what the congregation did, the audience would listen. She would often lead music and Brad would play the piano. When he played his solo's she was proud. When he looked at her she was happy and when he held her she was complete and safe. The connection was so easy. There were no fights no sad feelings and no disagreements.

The end came too soon though. He had to leave. She didn't want him to go, but something told her that she needed to let him grow even more. She read that setting those you love free is the only way for that growth to occur so with great reluctance, she let him go. To be honest, she had always thought that idea of letting go was stupid. But she had no choice this time. The last night she gave him a poem. She didn't find all the right words to say but she said it all at the end, when she wrote.

And if I have to prove my love is true
I would go to hell to be with you

She cried the night he left. She had told him that she thought she was preparing him for someone else. She didn't believe it, but she thought that by saying it, things would be easier. They weren't and even in retrospect it was still the most difficult night of her life.

As she read the letter she was confused by the part that said she need not respond. But more intriguing was the part that said there paths would cross again, didn't they always.

She remembered. Brad was right.

In fact, it was in College when their paths crossed again. She and Brad had stayed in touch for three years through the mail and through phone calls. Now he was visiting his parents and she was in college near by. She didn't recall exactly how he knew that but he drove up to see her.

Elaine set the letter down and seemed to go into a trance. Her mother had told her that she had crossed paths with her father several times before they finally were smart enough to get married. As she reflected on her life, Brad had crossed her path several times as well. Each time it seemed that this was the time. But then something, maybe fate, had intervened and something happened so that the paths could not unite.

Elaine found herself asking the question, is there really any such thing as a soul mate? Is there love?

In her case it did not seem so.

The tea was cold and the music was over. Rather than getting up, Elaine sat silently listening to the rain fall on the roof. She tried to hear a rhythm in the drops but after a few minutes realized that there was none. She looked again at the discarded letter on the couch. It was always the same. She would get the letter, read it and then remember her younger days. Most importantly she would always remember the talk she and her mother had that night after the dream. They seemed so close. Since that time they had grown apart. Was it because Brad had never returned to her? Everyone thought she and he were soul mates, even her mother. And now, this letter! Why is such a little thing causing such a tremendous impact in her life at this moment? Wait. She remembered.

Elaine got up from the couch and leaving the letter strewn on the middle pillow, she ran to her bedroom. It was in her private drawer that she kept the most special of all her memories. This memory was given to her the night that Brad said goodbye. It was the last poem that he wrote for her.

Life Story

A Poem of Existence

Pre-existence

We played amongst the stars
you and I
before our mortal life
with thousands of other spirits
shifting from plane to plane
spheres of existence
knowing all that we could know
for the time at hand

the bond between us was real
and energy encircled those we touched
not knowing futures
nor living pasts,
eternal in our nature
the symbol of love from our father and mother
totems to the galaxies
we were not yet one

the limitations grew too quickly
became to much
knowing this we could not progress
nor could we fail
amid stagnation we too were stopped
growth and reason no longer
came to us
and even though we were together
we needed more

we began the journey
but unlike our times together
this path would be taken alone
and even so
you promised that you would find me
and I you
and you were gone

Birth

there is no past and what is this place
strangers touch me
I have no sense
from darkness to this light
I hear myself crying
see myself confused
the shroud of the past has quickly fallen into place
I remember nothing
so far from you

this pain that touches me
where did it come from?
why am I here?
I think yet can not speak
I see but do not understand
so much has changed
the shroud enfolds me
goodbye

Childhood

The sun is warm, the days are full
and as I walk through misty mountains
the grasses teach me
the birds take flight
soaring to the heavens
as a child,
how I wish that I could fly

the water runs smoothly over my hand
I feel so much a part of all of this
why do I not understand?
my parents say I am quite rare
often alone, always with nature
strange to share
stranger yet to even discuss
because my points of view come not from here

I grow each year
yet feel further distant
what does this mean?
am I so different?

my father loves to hunt and fish
(I cannot kill an animal)
my friends engage in battles daily
(I am a man of peace)
my family follows only certain paths
based on religious fervor
(my mind,
expands beyond the dogmas of one belief
for there is truth in all things)
I am not part of this
and yet
they love me

Dan Clark

as a child I had a dream
my mission was to go to earth
and find you
and bring you back to heaven
I miss you

ah love,
what is it?
child to parent, parent to child
a godly gift and pure enough
but so many times have I fallen was it real? - only once
and if not real, why must we be mislead so often
or do we learn each time we try?

I found love
so unexpected, I was so young
she younger still
with but six months joined,
we had no idea
it should have been forever
and so
events derailed what was meant to be
she was the dawn
of all things

and as I grew
I saw her again
separate times, different stages
the bond remained
and yet
we did not act
this love so pure
born when so young
had lived for a score of earthly years
and deep inside
I knew not why

youth was given and youth had passed
the teachings of the world
out grew the spirits' search
and even as a teacher of god
something was amiss

Adulthood

the shroud is darker now
I am further from you
with work and wives and life
there is no time for searching
life's reality hits hard
a world's pain embraces all
there is no resolution
as wars prevail and nature dies
people cease to be what God intended

it seems the longer in the journey that we remain
the harder it is that truth unfold
what we originally had thought has passed
new gods arise
where old beliefs held true
and what we call adulthood
has led me far from you
out of touch with eternity
And that early promise made
has become a memory
hope is lost

Dan Clark

Finality

it is dark outside
the world has ended

the flickering light of hope
has truly descended into the abyss
spirits of ages past
so long a part of all
have abandoned this earth
the sun no longer rises
and children dream no more
I see no future for the common
I feel no love from God
the world rends, rejecting man
and deep within my soul
I long for younger days

Rebirth

and yet
within the deepest recesses of my heart
a candle burns
and there is belief that good shall reign
again upon this earth
a vision quest determines all
and hope begins to stir
the study on a spiritual plane
convinces me that there is more
and that in this darkest hour
a memory creeps back into my being
and reality is not what I thought it was
it is what I once knew
it's based in god and spirits being
reality is you

Eternity

it seemed forever and forever lost
through trials and tribulations
yet the medicine wheel of ancient pasts
the four corners of existence
all come flowing back to me
and now I know my place
a man of peace, of hope, of love
a teacher, a healer

as I draw nearer to the flame
the shroud evaporates completely
and all I see
is you
the dawning of my life
a promise fulfilled
and now

we play among the stars
you and I
our mortal life complete
the mating of our souls
so many lifetimes earlier
withstood the tests of time
and as our parents deemed so true
the stars and angels sing in gratefulness
we found each other
again

Every time Elaine read the words she thought to herself that this poem was finally the recognition that she and Brad were soul mates. She certainly knew it and she thought that he did too. So why were they still apart?

She grabbed the poem and returned to the sofa. There with the letter next to her, she unfolded the poem and re read the last lines;

you and I
our mortal life complete
the mating of our souls
so many lifetimes earlier
withstood the tests of time
and as our parents deemed so true
the stars and angels sing in gratefulness
we found each other
again

Her heart burst with joy and warmth and the tears began to stream
down her cheeks. She still loved this person and now she knew why
she felt so alone.

Chapter 10
October 1972

It was October. The leaves were changing on all the trees. The wind was light and the day was crisp. It was a perfect rocky mountain fall day. They had made arrangements to meet in the park near the college. Her last class was at 3:00 o'clock so she would meet him there around 3:30.

The hours seemed to take an eternity. Her last class, humanities, was always one of her favorites, but today she wanted nothing more that to see the clock say 3:00 and have the door close behind her. It had been so long and she wondered how the meeting would go. She was nervous but then again maybe she wasn't. She did know that she wanted to see Brad.

After three years and all the letters and calls, she wanted to see his face. She wanted him to look into her soul. She even wanted to make love to him. How could she be nervous?

This was the love of her life after all.

She left her last class, dropped her books off with Teri and headed down the hill. It was a short walk to the park. You would think a thousand different things would have gone through her mind at a time like this but nothing did. Not even the remote idea that he wouldn't be there.

She turned the corner and saw the park. There on the bench was a nineteen year old teenage boy. She knew before she saw him that it was Brad. She wanted to run right to him, but she walked. It seemed like forever and when she finally did reach him, she went straight into his embrace. The natural and only way to say hello! She stayed there for an eternity and that old feeling of safety and peace came over her again.

They talked until the park closed and the park ranger asked them to leave. He did so quite nicely, mentioning the fact that even for two love birds the park needed to close. They left the park had dinner and then Elaine wanted Brad to see her friends.

Back at the dorm's lobby, Elaine's friends had assembled. They needed to see this person that had had such an effect on Elaine. Teri had brought them all up to speed so that when Elaine and Brad arrived it was like a family reunion.

Elaine looked around at how easy it was for her friends and Brad to get along. Sure, he knew several of them, but even so, he was new to more than half. But he fit right in and everyone was enjoying the get together. Teri even asked if he had kept writing. Brad had answered that he lost his inspiration, so he was taking a break for a while.

It was getting late and Brad had to get a room at the hotel. He asked if Elaine wanted to help him check in. She agreed and they left. As there was only one hotel close to campus and Elaine had to be back by 11:00, Brad checked in there. He had hoped to see Elaine in the morning before he headed back to his parents house.

Brad checked into his room and he and Elaine talked for an hour. Something told him to ask her to stay and something told her to say yes, but the question did not come so the answer was not used. Brad drove Elaine back to the dorm and with a kiss goodnight went back to the hotel.

Brad left the next morning. Briefly seeing Elaine before her first class, she kissed him goodbye and wondered if she would ever see him again.

It wasn't long. A year later, Brad moved back to live with his parents and one weekend she decided to visit them. It was a total surprise.

Brad had moved back with his parents because he had decided to become a missionary. All along he had a spiritual side that few people saw, but the feelings were strong and he knew that if he did not do in then, it would never happen. He gave up a promising job and went home to prepare.

Brad had been engaged to a girl in Arizona for about a year. In fact, after his last trip up to see Elaine, he and Kathy had broken up. He didn't know why, it just didn't feel right. Now he was going on a mission for two years and there would be no girls in his life.

Seemed that no one ever could satisfy him! They were too tall or too short. They talked too much or not enough. They had too short of hair or they were over weight. They couldn't sing and they didn't like his poetry. Not one was perfect. Not one was, well, not one was Elaine.

Brad was working that Saturday when the office phone rang. Elaine said.

"Hello, is this Brad?"

"Of course it is Elaine. How did you know I was at work? And how on earth did you get this number?"

Elaine laughed, "Your mom silly. She always liked me anyway you know."

"Yes I remember." Brad acknowledged. "So what's up? How are you? How is school?"

"Well, let's see. School is fine. The sky is up and in about two minutes you can tell me how I am."

With that, Elaine walked right into the store and gave Brad the biggest hug he had had in several years.

"Wow, what a great surprise. I didn't know you were coming. What on earth?"

"Brad, you know I like surprises. Besides in a month you're off to Japan on your mission and I won't get to see you for a while. So I took the weekend off. Rode down with a friend and plan on staying until Sunday evening, when I have to go back."

"So where are you staying and can I see you?" Brad asked, forgetting all about the date he had that night.

"I think you will see me, your mom has invited me to stay at your house. Hope you don't mind."

"Mind, of course I don't mind. But there is one thing. I kind of have a date tonight. I promise I won't stay out late."

"Don't worry Brad I will talk with your sister until you get home. Just make sure not to fall in love with this girl." Elaine laughed and Brad noticed the twinkle in her eye. "Remember, I am yours and you are mine" Elaine said with a smile. "I haven't forgotten and you should not forget either."

After the date, Brad sat down in the kitchen to drink some water. Out of his sisters bedroom came Elaine. Dressed in a grandma night gown, very decent, she sat right down and asked how the date went. It was as if Elaine belonged in that chair asking that question. There was no jealousy in her voice. The strength of her hearts commitment overcame all doubts even those as real as a rival.

"How do you think?" Brad retorted. "All I could think about was you being here and talking to my sister. I'm sure she told you some stories."

"She did. But you know what? I want to hear them all from you."

"Gee, where do I start?" Brad thought out loud. He wanted to tell Elaine everything. A lot had happened. He had continued writing and even won an award or two. He was active in several sports and did quite well. In school he was elected vice president of student counsel. He had had a lot of friends and even several girl friends. He was engaged for a while but that didn't work out. He was no longer a virgin and even if it was with his fiancé he knew that Elaine was reserved in the area of sex before marriage. Worse, his fiance had gotten pregnant and they chose to have an abortion. It seemed right at the time, and even now, Brad thought it was the best decision, but how would Elaine take it?

Brad also wanted to tell her that he was losing his commitment to soul mates and eternal love. He had always thought Elaine was his, but with his moving all the time and now leaving on a mission, he new she would not be available when he got back. He wasn't going to ask her to wait. He had the mistaken opinion that he wanted to focus on his mission and thoughts of a beautiful girl waiting for him would distract him.

There was so much for him to tell her and so little time. Where does he start?

They began talking and talked for what seemed like hours. Unfortunately it was only minutes until they heard Brad's mothers voice saying;

"Hey you two, it's late. Time for bed, please!"

Brad grabbed Elaine's hand and walked her to her parent's bedroom.

"Is it okay if we come in for a moment mom?" Brad asked

"Sure son. What is it?"

"Well, it's this bed thing. Elaine and I were kind of hoping to not go to bed until we got married. Unless of course you think we should go ahead and go to bed right now."

"That's not what I meant," Lidia said in mock disgust. "Now go to bed! And alone!"

Brad and Elaine went back into the hall laughing. A quick hug good night and then each slipped into their separate rooms.

They both enjoyed the Sunday morning together and Brad drove Elaine back to the local university where she was going to meet her ride back to college. This time, as Elaine moved to kiss Brad goodbye, he turned his lips away and offered his cheek. Even though she was shocked, she kissed him goodbye and left the car. She didn't know what to think about that as it was so unlike Brad. But she knew she would see him again and thought to herself to ask him on that occasion.

Chapter 11
July 2008

The two years of his mission had gone by quickly. Elaine had a friend who was in the same place in Japan and he kept her abreast of Brad's progress. Brad was quite good, seemed to love the work and learned Japanese very quickly. He made a big impression on the missionaries, the members of the church and the people themselves. He had a number of converts and rose quickly in the organization. It seemed that the more responsibility he obtained, the more success he had.

Elaine was proud of those accomplishments. She had known he would be successful. She missed him, and not writing to him directly, but she respected his focus and didn't want to be a distraction. Besides, she knew he would be hers when he got home.

A couple of years later she received an invitation to his wedding. He had found someone else. Elaine was devastated. She cried for several days and even her mother could not console her. Then a very strange thing happened to her.

Elaine was rereading one of Brad's poems and she had fallen asleep. During the sleep she dreamt that she was walking in a forest all alone. During the walk she had come across several different cottages. Each cottage had a warm and enticing aroma or open door. Yet as she walked along the path she passed each door and left each cottage without entering. Then as she neared the end of the forest she noticed one last cottage.

As she neared the cottage, there was a man standing outside with a smile.

"Hi Elaine" he said.

"Brad?" "It is you, isn't it?"

Elaine ran to his arms and they held each other. As they were so embraced the forest turned into a pathway of clouds leading into the sky. In the distance, Elaine saw the very same city she had dreamt of years before and in an instant she was in the very same line that she was in before. This time, however, she was able to stay and with Brad at her side, she was able to enter and here the lessons of the Master.

Elaine awoke with a great sense of calm. She knew in her heart once again, that she and Brad were meant to be together and that at the right time, their paths would cross, they would find each other and forever embrace.

She got married shortly thereafter. Her marriage had lasted only 6 months. Now her present husband, to whom she had been married for nearly 20 years, knew nothing of Brad and that part of her life. She was still unsure that she wanted to tell him.

The record was over so she arose and against all logic put on Barry Manilow again. She sat for another hour before getting up, putting the letter in its envelope, and sliding it into the desk. She changed the music to Bach.

She had done the same routine at least a hundred times since receiving the letter.

Wondering whether she should write or not. Wondering what the feelings meant. Wondering if she dared to hope? Remembering what her mother had told her about soul mates and eternal love.

What about her family. She could never leave them, could she? Did he want her to?

What did it all mean? Was she trying to put too much meaning into a simple gesture? A hundred, no a thousand questions arose. No answers, and there would be none, unless she responded to the letter.

So, today was different. She was finally getting around to doing what she should have done several months ago. She picked out the letter, re-read it again, felt the same warm peaceful feelings she always felt. She looked for pen and paper. She put on Barry Manilow, then, looking one last time at the picture of her husband and family she began to write,

Dearest Brad........................

Chapter 12

Saturday

It had been over a year since Elaine had received the letter from Brad. Today, listening to Manilow and turning to page 117 of the very same book about star crossed lovers, she takes a moment to look out the front window of her new apartment.

The deep blue water of the bay is a beautiful contrast to the green of the hills that surrounded this inlet. The crystal blue sky a bright change from the usual gray morning drizzle she had grown up with. As she watched the international freighter enter the harbor she glanced at the country side and could not remember anything as peaceful or precious. The cherry blossoms were in full bloom and just like the neighbors said, this was the most beautiful spring Tokyo had ever experienced.

EPILOGUE

And finally, as Elaine and Brad begin their earthly lives together, they leave you with:

The Gift

Oft times we wonder,
and yet,
   are left unaware
Having given so many times;
again
left with nothing
But now,
   the greatest gift of all;
      beyond the memories of the past
      has blessed our lives;
Respectively given,
each to the other
we now share with you
   our truest friends
      That humble offering;
      So sublime; as to not be seen
      Yet so strong; as to turn the heart;
And with this gift,
may all your days becomes
as our lives already are

         ....filled with love!

Printed in the United States
by Baker & Taylor Publisher Services

Printed in the United States
by Baker & Taylor Publisher Services